THE TOMB'S SECRET

BY

ROBERT E. HOWARD

British Library Cataloguing-in-Publication Data
A catalogue record for this book is available from the
British Library

Robert E. Howard

Robert Ervin Howard was born in Peaster, Texas in 1906. During his youth, his family moved between a variety of Texan boomtowns, and Howard – a bookish and somewhat introverted child – was steeped in the violent myths and legends of the Old South. Although he loved reading and learning, Howard developed a distinctly Texan, hardboiled outlook on the world. He became a passionate fan of boxing, taking it up at an amateur level, and from the age of nine began to write adventure tales of semi-historical bloodshed. In 1919, when Howard was thirteen, his family moved to the Central Texas hamlet of Cross Plains, where he would stay for the rest of his life.

At fifteen Howard began to read the pulp magazines of the day, and to write more seriously. The December 1922 issue of his high school newspaper featured two of his stories, 'Golden Hope Christmas' and 'West is West'. In 1924 he sold his first piece – a short caveman tale titled 'Spear and Fang' – for $16 to the not-yet-famous *Weird Tales* magazine. He published with the magazine regularly over the next few years. 1929 was a breakout year for Howard, in that the 23-year-old writer began to sell to other magazines, such as *Ghost Stories* and *Argosy*, both of whom had previously sent him hundreds of rejection slips. In 1930, he began a

1

correspondence with weird fiction master H. P. Lovecraft which ran up to his death six years later, and is regarded as one of the great correspondence cycles in all of fantasy literature.

It was partly due to Lovecraft's encouragement that Howard created his most famous character, Conan the Cimmerian. Conan – a barbarian-turned-King during the Hyborian Age, a mythical period of some 12,000 years ago – featured in seventeen *Weird Tales* stories between 1933 and 1936, and is now regarded as having spawned the 'sword and sorcery' genre, making Howard's influence on fantasy literature comparable to that of J. R. R. Tolkien's. The Conan stories have since been adapted many times, most famously in the series of films starring Arnold Schwarzenegger.

Howard was enjoying an all-time high in sales by the beginning of 1936, but he was also deeply upset by the ill health of his mother, who had fallen into a coma. On the morning of June 11, 1936, he asked an attending nurse whether she would ever recover, and the nurse replied negatively. Howard walked to his car, parked outside the family home in Cross Plains, and shot himself. He died eight hours later, aged just thirty

When James Willoughby, millionaire philanthropist, realized that the dark, lightless car was deliberately crowding him into the curb, he acted with desperate decision. Snapping off his own lights, he threw open the door on the opposite side from the onrushing stranger, and leaped out, without stopping his own car. He landed sprawling on all fours, shredding the knees of his trousers and tearing the skin on his hands. An instant later his auto crashed cataclysmically into the curb, and the crunch of crumpled fenders and the tinkle of breaking glass mingled with the deafening reverberation of a sawed-off shotgun as the occupants of the mysterious car, not yet realizing that their intended victim had deserted his automobile, blasted the machine he had just left.

Before the echoes died away, Willoughby was up and running through the darkness with an energy remarkable for his years. He knew that his ruse was already discovered, but it takes longer to swing a big car around than for a desperately frightened man to burst through a hedge, and a flitting figure in the darkness is a poor target. So James Willoughby lived where others had died, and presently came on foot and in disheveled condition to his home, which adjoined the park beside which the murderous attempt had been made. The police, hastening to his call, found him in a condition of mingled fear and bewilderment. He had seen none of his attackers; he could give no reason for the attack. All that he seemed to know was that death had struck at him from the dark, suddenly, terribly and mysteriously.

It was only reasonable to suppose that death would strike again at its chosen victim, and that was why Brock Rollins, detective, kept a rendezvous the next evening with one Joey Glick, a nondescript character of the underworld who served his purpose in the tangled scheme of things.

Rollins bulked big in the dingy back-room appointed for the meeting. His massive shoulders and thick body dwarfed his height. His cold blue eyes contrasted with the thick black hair that crowned his low broad forehead, and his civilized garments could not conceal the almost savage muscularity of his hard frame.

Opposite him Joey Glick, never an impressive figure, looked even more insignificant than usual. And Joey's skin was a pasty grey, and Joey's fingers shook as he fumbled with a bit of paper on which was drawn a peculiar design.

"Somebody planted it on me," he chattered. "Right after I phoned you. In the jamb on the uptown train. Me, Joey Glick! They plant it on me and I don't even know it. Only one man in this burg handles dips that slick--even if I didn't know already.

"Look! It's the death-blossom! The symbol of the Sons of Erlik! They're after me! They've been shadowing me-- tapping wires. They know I know too much--"

"Come to the point, will you?" grunted Rollins "You said you had a tip about the gorillas who tried to put the finger on Jim Willoughby. Quit shaking and spill it. And tell me, cold turkey--who was it?"

"The man behind it is Yarghouz Barolass."

Rollins grunted in some surprise.

"I didn't know murder was his racket."

"Wait!" Joey babbled, so scared he was scarcely coherent. His brain was addled, his speech disjointed. "He's head of the American branch of the Sons of Erlik--I know he is--"

"Chinese?"

"He's a Mongol. His racket is blackmailing nutty old dames who fall for his black magic. You know that. But this is bigger. Listen, you know about Richard Lynch?"

"Sure; got smashed up in an auto wreck by a hit-and-run speed maniac a week ago. Lay unidentified in a morgue all night before they discovered who he was. Some crazy loon tried to steal the corpse off the slab. What's that got to do with Willoughby?"

"It wasn't an accident." Joey was fumbling for a cigarette. "They meant to get him--Yarghouz's mob. It was them after the body that night--"

"Have you been hitting the pipe?" demanded Rollins harshly.

"No, damn it!" shrilled Joey. "I tell you, Yarghouz was after Richard Lynch's corpse, just like he's sending his mob after Job Hopkins' body tomorrow night--"

"What?" Rollins came erect, glaring incredulously.

"Don't rush me," begged Joey, striking a match. "Gimme time. That death-blossom has got me jumping sideways. I'm jittery--"

"I'll say you are," grunted Rollins. "You've been babbling a lot of stuff that don't mean anything, except it's Yarghouz Barolass who had Lynch bumped off, and now is after Willoughby. Why? That's what I want to know. Straighten it out and give me the low-down."

"Alright," promised Joey, sucking avidly at his cigarette. "Lemme have a drag. I been so upset I haven't even smoked since I reached into my pocket for a fag and found that damned death-flower. This is straight goods. I know why they want the bodies of Richard Lynch, Job Hopkins and James Willoughby--"

With appalling suddenness his hands shot to his throat, crushing the smoldering cigarette in his fingers. His eyes distended, his face purpled. Without a word he swayed upright, reeled and crashed to the floor. With a curse Rollins sprang up, bent over him, ran skilled hands over his body.

"Dead as Judas Iscariot," swore the detective. "What an infernal break! I knew his heart would get him some day, if he kept hitting the pipe--"

He halted suddenly. On the floor where it had fallen beside the dead man lay the bit of ornamented paper Joey had called the blossom of death, and beside it lay a crumpled package of cigarettes.

"When did he change his brand?" muttered Rollins. "He never smoked any kind but a special Egyptian make before; never saw him use this brand." He lifted the package, drew out a cigarette and broke it into his hand, smelling the contents gingerly. There was a faint but definite odor which was not part of the smell of the cheap tobacco.

"The fellow who slipped that death-blossom into his pocket could have shifted fags on him just as easy," muttered the detective. "They must have known he was coming here to talk to me. But the question is, how much do they know now? They can't know how much or how little he told me. They evidently didn't figure on him reaching me at all--thought he'd take a draw before he got here. Ordinarily he would have; but this time he was too scared even to remember to smoke. He needed dope, not tobacco, to steady his nerve."

Going to the door, he called softly. A stocky bald-headed man answered his call, wiping his hands on a dirty apron. At the sight of the crumpled body he recoiled, paling.

"Heart attack, Spike," grunted Rollins. "See that he gets what's needed." And the big dick thrust a handful of crumpled bills into Spike's fingers as he strode forth. A hard man, Rollins, but one mindful of his debts to the dead as well as the living.

A few minutes later be was crouched over a telephone. "This you, Hoolihan?"

A voice booming back over the wires assured him that the chief of police was indeed at the other end.

"What killed Job Hopkins?" he asked abruptly.

"Why, heart attack, I understand." There was some surprise in the chief's voice. "Passed out suddenly, day before yesterday, while smoking his after-dinner cigar, according to the papers. Why?"

"Who's guarding Willoughby?" demanded Rollins without answering.

"Laveaux, Hanson, McFarlane and Harper. But I don't see--"

"Not enough," snapped Rollins. "Beat it over there yourself with three or four more men."

"Say, listen here, Rollins!" came back the irate bellow. "Are you telling _me_ how to run my business?"

"Right now I am." Rollins' cold hard grin was almost tangible in his voice. "This happens to be in my particular domain. We're not fighting white men; it's a gang of River Street yellow-bellies who've put Willoughby on the spot. I won't say any more right now. There's been too damned much wire-tapping in this burg. But you beat it over to Willoughby's as fast as you can get there. Don't let him out of your sight. Don't let him smoke, eat or drink anything till I get there. I'll be right on over."

"Okay," came the answer over the wires. "You've been working the River Street quarter long enough to know what you're doing."

Rollins snapped the receiver back on its hook and strode out into the misty dimness of River Street, with its furtive hurrying forms--stooped alien figures which would have fitted less incongruously into the scheme of Canton, Bombay or Stamboul.

The big dick walked with a stride even springier than usual, a more aggressive lurch of his massive shoulders. That betokened unusual wariness, a tension of nerves. He knew that he was a marked man, since his talk with Joey Glick. He did not try to fool himself; it was certain that the spies of the man he was fighting knew that Joey had reached him before he died. The fact that they could not know just how much the fellow had told before he died, would make them all the more dangerous. He did not underestimate his own position. He knew that if there was one man in the city capable of dealing with Yarghouz Barolass, it was himself, with his experience gained from years of puzzling through the devious and often grisly mysteries of River Street, with its swarms of brown and yellow inhabitants.

"Taxi?" A cab drew purring up beside the curb, anticipating his summoning gesture. The driver did not lean out into the light of the street. His cap seemed to be drawn low, not unnaturally so, but, standing on the sidewalk, it was impossible for the detective to tell whether or not he was a white man.

"Sure," grunted Rollins, swinging open the door and climbing in. "540 Park Place, and step on it."

The taxi roared through the crawling traffic, down shadowy River Street, wheeled off onto 35th Avenue, crossed over, and sped down a narrow side street.

"Taking a short cut?" asked the detective.

"Yes, sir." The driver did not look back. His voice ended in a sudden hissing intake of breath. There was no partition between the front and back seats. Rollins was leaning forward, his gun jammed between the shoulders of the driver.

"Take the next right-hand turn and drive to the address I gave you," he said softly. "Think I can't tell the back of a yellow neck by the street lamp? You drive, but you drive careful. If you try to wreck us, I'll fill you full of lead before you can twist that wheel. No monkey business now; you wouldn't be the first man I've plugged in the course of duty."

The driver twisted his head about to stare briefly into the grim face of his captor; his wide thin mouth gaped, his coppery features were ashy. Not for nothing had Rollins established his reputation as a man-hunter among the sinister denizens of the Oriental quarter.

"Joey was right," muttered Rollins between his teeth. "I don't know your name, but I've seen you hanging around Yarghouz Barolass's joint when he had it over on Levant Street. You won't take me for a ride, not tonight. I know that trick, old copper-face. You'd have a flat, or run out of gas at some convenient spot. Any excuse for you to get out of the car and out of range while a hatchet-man hidden somewhere mows me down with a sawed-off. You better hope none of your friends see us and try anything, because this gat has a hair-trigger, and it's cocked. I couldn't die quick enough not to pull the trigger."

The rest of that grim ride was made in silence, until the reaches of South Park rose to view--darkened, except for a fringe of lights around the boundaries, because of municipal economy which sought to reduce the light bill.

"Swing into the park," ordered Rollins, as they drove along the street which passed the park, and, further on, James Willoughby's house. "Cut off your lights, and drive as I tell you. You can feel your way between the trees."

The darkened car glided into a dense grove and came to a halt. Rollins fumbled in his pockets with his left hand and drew out a small flashlight, and a pair of handcuffs. In climbing out, he was forced to remove his muzzle from close contact with his prisoner's back, but the gun menaced the Mongol in the small ring of light emanating from the flash.

"Climb out," ordered the detective. "That's right--slow and easy. You're going to have to stay here awhile. I didn't want to take you to the station right now, for several reasons. One of them is I didn't want your pals to know I turned the tables on you. I'm hoping they'll still be patiently waiting for you to bring me into range of their sawed-offs--ha, would you?"

The Mongol, with a desperate wrench, struck the flashlight from the detective's hand, plunging them into darkness.

Rollins' clutching fingers locked like a vise on his adversary's coat sleeve, and at the same instant he instinctively threw out his .45 before his belly, to parry the stroke he knew would instantly come. A knife clashed venomously against the blue steel cylinder, and Rollins hooked his foot about an ankle and jerked powerfully. The fighters went down together, and the knife sliced the detective's coat as they fell. Then his blindingly driven gun barrel crunched glancingly against a shaven skull, and the straining form went limp.

Panting and swearing beneath his breath, Rollins retrieved the flashlight and cuffs, and set to work securing his prisoner. The Mongol was completely out; it was no light matter to stop a full-arm swing from Brock Rollins. Had the blow landed solidly it would have caved in the skull like an egg-shell.

Handcuffed, gagged with strips torn from his coat, and his feet bound with the same material, the Mongol was placed in the car, and Rollins turned and strode through the shadows of the park, toward the eastern hedge beyond which lay James Willoughby's estate. He hoped that this affair would give him some slight advantage in this blind battle. While the Mongols waited for him to ride into the trap they had undoubtedly laid for him somewhere in the city, perhaps he could do a little scouting unmolested.

James Willoughby's estate adjoined South Park on the east. Only a high hedge separated the park from his grounds. The big three-storied house--disproportionately huge for a bachelor--towered among carefully trimmed trees and shrubbery, amidst a level, shaven lawn. There were lights in the two lower floors, none in the third. Rollins knew that Willoughby's study was a big room on the second floor, on the west side of the house. From that room no light issued between the heavy shutters. Evidently curtains and shades were drawn inside. The big dick grunted in approval as he stood looking through the hedge.

He knew that a plainclothes man was watching the house from each side, and he marked the bunch of shrubbery amidst which would be crouching the man detailed to guard the west side. Craning his neck, he saw a car in front of the house, which faced south, and he knew it to be that of Chief Hoolihan.

With the intention of taking a short cut across the lawn he wormed through the hedge, and, not wishing to be shot by mistake, he called softly: "Hey, Harper!"

There was no answer. Rollins strode toward the shrubbery.

"Asleep at the post?" he muttered angrily. "Eh, what's this?"

He had stumbled over something in the shadows of the shrubs. His hurriedly directed beam shone on the white, upturned face of a man. Blood dabbled the features, and a crumpled hat lay near by, an unfired pistol near the limp hand.

"Knocked stiff from behind!" muttered Rollins. "What--"

Parting the shrub he gazed toward the house. On that side an ornamental chimney rose tier by tier, until it towered above the roof. And his eyes became slits as they centered on a window on the third floor within easy reach of that chimney. On all other windows the shutters were closed; but these stood open.

With frantic haste he tore through the shrubbery and ran across the lawn, stooping like a bulky bear, amazingly fleet for one of his weight. As he rounded the corner of the house and rushed toward the steps, a man rose swiftly from among the hedges lining the walk, and covered him, only to lower his gun with an exclamation of recognition.

"Where's Hoolihan?" snapped the detective.

"Upstairs with old man Willoughby. What's up?"

"Harper's been slugged," snarled Rollins. "Beat it out there; you know where he was posted. Wait there until I call you. If you see anything you don't recognize trying to leave the house, plug it! I'll send out a man to take your place here."

He entered the front door and saw four men in plain clothes lounging about in the main hall.

"Jackson," he snapped, "take Hanson's place out in front. I sent him around to the west side. The rest of you stand by for anything."

Mounting the stair in haste, he entered the study on the second floor, breathing a sigh of relief as he found the occupants apparently undisturbed.

The curtains were closely drawn over the windows, and only the door letting into the hall was open. Willoughby was there, a tall spare man, with a scimitar sweep of nose and a bony aggressive chin. Chief Hoolihan, big, bear-like, rubicund, boomed a greeting.

"All your men downstairs?" asked Rollins.

"Sure; nothin' can get past 'em and I'm stayin' here with Mr. Willoughby--"

"And in a few minutes more you'd both have been scratching gravel in Hell," snapped Rollins. "Didn't I tell you we were dealing with Orientals? You concentrated all your force below, never thinking that death might slip in on you from above. But I haven't time to turn out that light. Mr. Willoughby, get over there in that alcove. Chief, stand in front of him, and watch that door that leads into the hall. I'm going to leave it open. Locking it would be useless, against what we're fighting. If anything you don't recognize comes through it, shoot to kill."

"What the devil are you driving at, Rollins?" demanded Hoolihan.

"I mean one of Yarghouz Barolass's killers is in this house!" snapped Rollins. "There may be more than one; anyway, he's somewhere upstairs. Is this the only stair, Mr. Willoughby? No back-stair?"

"This is the only one in the house," answered the millionaire. "There are only bedrooms on the third floor."

"Where's the light button for the hall on that floor?"

"At the head of the stairs, on the left; but you aren't--"

"Take your places and do as I say," grunted Rollins, gliding out into the hallway.

He stood glaring at the stair which wound up above him, its upper part masked in shadow. Somewhere up there lurked a soulless slayer--a Mongol killer, trained in the art of murder, who lived only to perform his master's will. Rollins started to call the men below, then changed his mind. To raise his voice would be to warn the lurking murderer above. Setting his teeth, he glided up the stair. Aware that he was limned in the light below, he realized the desperate recklessness of his action; but he had long ago learned that he could not match subtlety against the Orient. Direct action, however desperate, was always his best bet. He did not fear a bullet as he charged up; the Mongols preferred to slay in silence; but a thrown knife could kill as promptly as tearing lead. His one chance lay in the winding of the stair.

He took the last steps with a thundering rush, not daring to use his flash, plunged into the gloom of the upper hallway, frantically sweeping the wall for the light button. Even as he felt life and movement in the darkness beside him, his groping fingers found it. The scrape of a foot on the floor beside him galvanized him, and as he instinctively flinched back, something whined past his breast and thudded deep into the wall. Then under his frenzied fingers, light flooded the hall.

Almost touching him, half crouching, a copper-skinned giant with a shaven head wrenched at a curved knife which was sunk deep in the woodwork. He threw up his head, dazzled by the light, baring yellow fangs in a bestial snarl.

Rollins had just left a lighted area. His eyes accustomed themselves more swiftly to the sudden radiance. He threw his left like a hammer at the Mongol's jaw. The killer swayed and fell out cold.

Hoolilhan was bellowing from below.

"Hold everything," answered Rollins. "Send one of the boys up here with the cuffs. I'm going through these bedrooms."

Which he did, switching on the lights, gun ready, but finding no other lurking slayer. Evidently Yarghouz Barolass considered one would be enough. And so it might have been, but for the big detective.

Having latched all the shutters and fastened the windows securely, he returned to the study, whither the prisoner had been taken. The man had recovered his senses and sat, handcuffed, on a divan. Only the eyes, black and snaky, seemed alive in the copperish face.

"Mongol alright," muttered Rollins. "No Chinaman."

"What is all this?" complained Hoolihan, still upset by the realization that an invader had slipped through his cordon.

"Easy enough. This fellow sneaked up on Harper and laid him cold. Some of these fellows could steal the teeth right out of your mouth. With all those shrubs and trees it was a cinch. Say, send out a couple of the boys to bring in Harper, will you? Then he climbed that fancy chimney. That was a cinch, too. I could do it myself. Nobody had thought to fasten the shutters on that floor, because nobody expected an attack from that direction.

"Mr. Willoughby, do you know anything about Yarghouz Barolass?"

"I never heard of him," declared the philanthropist, and though Rollins scanned him narrowly, he was impressed by the ring of sincerity in Willoughby's voice.

"Well, he's a mystic fakir," said Rollins. "Hangs around Levant Street and preys on old ladies with more money than sense--faddists. Gets them interested in Taoism and Lamaism and then plays on their superstitions and blackmails them. I know his racket, but I've never been able to put the finger on him, because his victims won't squeal. But he's behind these attacks on you."

"Then why don't we go grab him?" demanded Hoolihan.

"Because we don't know where he is. He knows that I know he's mixed up in this. Joey Glick spilled it to me, just before he croaked. Yes, Joey's dead--poison; more of Yarghouz's work. By this time Yarghouz will have deserted his usual hang-outs, and be hiding somewhere--probably in some secret underground dive that we couldn't find in a hundred years, now that Joey is dead."

"Let's sweat it out of this yellow-belly," suggested Hoolihan.

Rollins grinned coldly. "You'd sweat to death yourself before he'd talk. There's another tied up in a car out in the park. Send a couple of boys after him, and you can try your hand on both of them. But you'll get damned little out of them. Come here, Hoolihan."

Drawing him aside, he said: "I'm sure that Job Hopkins was poisoned in the same manner they got Joey Glick. Do you remember anything unusual about the death of Richard Lynch?"

"Well, not about his death; but that night somebody apparently tried to steal and mutilate his corpse--"

"What do you mean, mutilate?" demanded Rollins.

"Well, a watchman heard a noise and went into the room and found Lynch's body on the floor, as if somebody had tried to carry it off, and then maybe got scared off. And a lot of the _teeth_ had been pulled or knocked out!"

"Well, I can't explain the teeth," grunted Rollins. "Maybe they were knocked out in the wreck that killed Lynch. But this is my hunch: Yarghouz Barolass is stealing the bodies of wealthy men, figuring on screwing a big price out of their families. When they don't die quick enough, he bumps them off."

Hoolihan cursed in shocked horror.

"But Willoughby hasn't any family."

"Well, I reckon they figure the executors of his estate will kick in. Now listen: I'm borrowing your car for a visit to Job Hopkins' vault. I got a tip that they're going to lift his corpse tomorrow night. I believe they'll spring it tonight, on the chance that I might have gotten the tip. I believe they'll try to get ahead of me. They may have already, what with all this delay. I figured on being out there long before now.

"No, I don't want any help. Your flat-feet are more of a hindrance than a help in a job like this. You stay here with Willoughby. Keep men upstairs as well as down. Don't let Willoughby open any packages that might come, don't even let him answer a phone call. I'm going to Hopkins' vault, and I don't know when I'll be back; may roost out there all night. It just depends on when--or if--they come for the corpse."

A few minutes later he was speeding down the road on his grim errand. The graveyard which contained the tomb of Job Hopkins was small, exclusive, where only the bones of rich men were laid to rest. The wind moaned through the cypress trees which bent shadow-arms above the gleaming marble.

Rollins approached from the back side, up a narrow, tree-lined side street. He left the car, climbed the wall, and stole through the gloom, beneath the pallid shafts, under the cypress shadows. Ahead of him Job Hopkins' tomb glimmered whitely. And he stopped short, crouching low in the shadows. He saw a glow--a spark of light--it was extinguished, and through the open door of the tomb trooped half a dozen shadowy forms. His hunch had been right, but they had gotten there ahead of him. Fierce anger sweeping him at the ghoulish crime, he leaped forward, shouting a savage command.

They scattered like rats, and his crashing volley re-echoed futilely among the sepulchers. Rushing forward recklessly, swearing savagely, he came into the tomb, and turning his light into the interior, winced at what he saw. The coffin had been burst open, but the tomb itself was not empty. In a careless heap on the floor lay the embalmed corpse of Job Hopkins--_and the lower jawbone had been sawed away._

"What the Hell!" Rollins stopped short, bewildered at the sudden disruption of his theory. "They didn't want the body. What did they want? His teeth? And they got Richard Lynch's teeth--"

Lifting the body back into its resting place, he hurried forth, shutting the door of the tomb behind him. The wind whined through the cypress, and mingled with it was a low moaning sound. Thinking that one of his shots had gone home, after all, he followed the noise, warily, pistol and flash ready.

The sound seemed to emanate from a bunch of low cedars near the wall, and among them he found a man lying. The beam revealed the stocky figure, the square, now convulsed face of a Mongol. The slant eyes were glazed, the back of the coat soaked with blood. The man was gasping his last, but Rollins found no trace of a bullet wound on him. In his back, between his shoulders, stood up the hilt of a curious skewer-like knife. The fingers of his right hand had been horribly gashed, as if he had sought to retain his grasp on something which his slayers desired.

"Running from me he bumped into somebody hiding among these cedars," muttered Rollins. "But who? And why? By God, Willoughby hasn't told me everything."

He stared uneasily at the crowding shadows. No stealthy shuffling footfall disturbed the sepulchral quiet. Only the wind whimpered through the cypress and the cedars. The detective was alone with the dead--with the corpses of rich men in their ornate tombs, and with the staring yellow man whose flesh was not yet rigid.

"You're back in a hurry," said Hoolihan, as Rollins entered the Willoughby study. "Do any good?"

"Did the yellow boys talk?" countered Rollins.

"They did not," growled the chief. "They sat like pot-bellied idols. I sent 'em to the station, along with Harper. He was still in a daze."

"Mr. Willoughby," Rollins sank down rather wearily into an arm-chair and fixed his cold gaze on the philanthropist, "am I right in believing that you and Richard Lynch and Job Hopkins were at one time connected with each other in some way?"

"Why do you ask?" parried Willoughby.

"Because somehow the three of you are connected in this matter. Lynch's death was not accidental, and I'm pretty sure that Job Hopkins was poisoned. Now the same gang is after you. I thought it was a body-snatching racket, but an apparent attempt to steal Richard Lynch's corpse out of the morgue, now seems to resolve itself into what was in reality a successful attempt to get his teeth. Tonight a gang of Mongols entered the tomb of Job Hopkins, obviously for the same purpose--"

A choking cry interrupted him. Willoughby sank back, his face livid.

"My God, after all these years!"

Rollins stiffened.

"Then you do know Yarghouz Barolass? You know why he's after you?"

Willoughby shook his head. "I never heard of Yarghouz Barolass before. But I know why they killed Lynch and Hopkins."

"Then you'd better spill the works," advised Rollins. "We're working in the dark as it is."

"I will!" The philanthropist was visibly shaken. He mopped his brow with a shaking hand, and reposed himself with an effort.

"Twenty years ago," he said, "Lynch, Hopkins and myself, young men just out of college, were in China, in the employ of the war-lord Yuen Chin. We were chemical engineers. Yuen Chin was a far-sighted man--ahead of his time, scientifically speaking. He visioned the day when men would war with gases and deadly chemicals. He supplied us with a splendid laboratory, in which to discover or invent some such element of destruction for his use.

"He paid us well; the foundations of all of our fortunes were laid there. We were young, poor, unscrupulous.

"More by chance than skill we stumbled onto a deadly secret--the formula for a poisonous gas, a thousand times more deadly than anything yet dreamed of. That was what he was paying us to invent or discover for him, but the discovery sobered us. We realized that the man who possessed the secret of that gas, could easily conquer the world. We were willing to aid Yuen Chin against his Mongolian enemies; we were not willing to elevate a yellow mandarin to world empire, to see our hellish discovery directed against the lives of our own people.

"Yet we were not willing to destroy the formula, because we foresaw a time when America, with her back to the wall, might have a desperate need for such a weapon. So we wrote out the formula in code, but left out three symbols, without any of which the formula is meaningless and undecipherable. Each of us then, had a lower jaw tooth pulled out, and on the gold tooth put in its place, was carved one of the three symbols. Thus we took precautions against our own greed, as well as against the avarice of outsiders. One of us might conceivably fall so low as to sell the secret, but it would be useless without the other two symbols.

"Yuen Chin fell and was beheaded on the great execution ground at Peking. We escaped, Lynch, Hopkins and I, not only with our lives but with most of the money which had been paid us. But the formula, scrawled on parchment, we were obliged to leave, secreted among musty archives in an ancient temple.

"Only one man knew our secret: an old Chinese tooth-puller, who aided us in the matter of the teeth. He owed his life to Richard Lynch, and when he swore the oath of eternal silence, we knew we could trust him."

"Yet you think somebody is after the secret symbols?"

"What else could it be? I cannot understand it. The old tooth-puller must have died long ago. Who could have learned of it? Torture would not have dragged the secret from him. Yet it can be for no other reason that this fellow you call Yarghouz Barolass murdered and mutilated the bodies of my former companions, and now is after me.

"Why, I love life as well as any man, but my own peril shrinks into insignificance compared to the world-wide menace contained in those little carven symbols--two of which are now, according to what you say, in the hands of some ruthless foe of the western world.

"Somebody has found the formula we left hidden in the temple, and has learned somehow of its secret. Anything can come out of China. Just now the bandit war-lord Yah Lai is threatening to overthrow the National government-- who knows what devilish concoction that Chinese caldron is brewing?

"The thought of the secret of that gas in the hands of some Oriental conqueror is appalling. My God, gentlemen, I fear you do not realize the full significance of the matter!"

"I've got a faint idea," grunted Rollins. "Ever see a dagger like this?" He presented the weapon that had killed the Mongol.

"Many of them, in China," answered Willoughby promptly.

"Then it isn't a Mongol weapon?"

"No; it's distinctly Chinese; there is a conventional Manchu inscription on the hilt."

"Ummmmmm!" Rollins sat scowling, chin on fist, idly tapping the blade against his shoe, lost in meditation. Admittedly, he was all at sea, lost in a bewildering tangle. To his companions he looked like a grim figure of retribution, brooding over the fate of the wicked. In reality he was cursing his luck.

"What are you going to do now?" demanded Hoolihan.

"Only one thing to do," responded Rollins. "I'm going to try to run down Yarghouz Barolass. I'm going to start with River Street--God knows, it'll be like looking for a rat in a swamp. I want you to contrive to let one of those Mongols escape, Hoolihan. I'll try to trail him back to Yarghouz's hangout--"

The phone tingled loudly.

Rollins reached it with a long stride.

"Who speaks, please?" Over the wire came a voice with a subtle but definite accent.

"Brock Rollins," grunted the big dick.

"A friend speaks, Detective," came the bland voice. "Before we progress further, let me warn you that it will be impossible to trace this call, and would do you no good to do so."

"Well?" Rollins was bristling like a big truculent dog.

"Mr. Willoughby," the suave voice continued, "is a doomed man. He is as good as dead already. Guards and guns will not save him, when the Sons of Erlik are ready to strike. But _you_ can save him, without firing a shot!"

"Yeah?" It was a scarcely articulate snarl humming bloodthirstily from Rollins' bull-throat.

"If you were to come alone to the House of Dreams on Levant street, Yarghouz Barolass would speak to you, and a compromise might be arranged whereby Mr. Willoughby's life would be spared."

"Compromise, Hell!" roared the big dick, the skin over his knuckles showing white. "Who do you think you're talking to? Think I'd fall into a trap like that?"

"You have a hostage," came back the voice. "One of the men you hold is Yarghouz Barolass's brother. Let him suffer if there is treachery. I swear by the bones of my ancestors, no harm shall come to you!"

The voice ceased with a click at the other end of the wire.

Rollins wheeled.

"Yarghouz Barolass must be getting desperate to try such a child's trick as that!" he swore. Then he considered, and muttered, half to himself: "By the bones of his ancestors! Never heard of a Mongolian breaking _that_ oath. All that stuff about Yarghouz's brother may be the bunk. Yet--well, maybe he's trying to outsmart me--draw me away from Willoughby--on the other hand, maybe he thinks that I'd never fall for a trick like that--aw, to Hell with thinking! I'm going to start acting!"

"What do you mean?" demanded Hoolihan.

"I mean I'm going to the House of Dreams, alone."

"You're crazy!" exclaimed Hoolihan. "Take a squad, surround the house, and raid it!"

"And find an empty rat-den," grunted Rollins, his peculiar obsession for working alone again asserting itself.

Dawn was not far away when Rollins entered the smoky den near the waterfront which was known to the Chinese as the House of Dreams, and whose dingy exterior masked a subterranean opium joint. Only a pudgy Chinaboy nodded behind the counter; he looked up with no apparent surprise. Without a word he led Rollins to a curtain in the back of the shop, pulled it aside, and revealed a door. The detective gripped his gun under his coat, nerves taut with excitement that must come to any man who has deliberately walked into what might prove to be a death-trap. The boy knocked, lifting a sing-song monotone, and a voice answered from within. Rollins started. He recognized that voice. The boy opened the door, bobbed his head and was gone. Rollins entered, pulling the door to behind him.

He was in a room heaped and strewn with divans and silk cushions. If there were other doors, they were masked by the black velvet hangings, which, worked with gilt dragons, covered the walls. On a divan near the further wall squatted a stocky, pot-bellied shape, in black silk, a close-fitting velvet cap on his shaven head.

"So you came, after all!" breathed the detective. "Don't move, Yarghouz Barolass. I've got you covered through my coat. Your gang can't get me quick enough to keep me from getting you first."

"Why do you threaten me, Detective?" Yarghouz Barolass's face was expressionless, the square, parchment-skinned face of a Mongol from the Gobi, with wide thin lips and glittering black eyes. His English was perfect.

"See, I trust you. I am here, alone. The boy who let you in said that you are alone. Good. You kept your word, I keep my promise. For the time there is truce between us, and I am ready to bargain, as you suggested."

"As _I_ suggested?" demanded Rollins.

"I have no desire to harm Mr. Willoughby, any more than I wished to harm either of the other gentlemen," said Yarghouz Barolass. "But knowing them all as I did--from report and discreet observation--it never occurred to me that I could obtain what I wished while they lived. So I did not enter into negotiations with them."

"So you want Willoughby's tooth, too?"

"Not I," disclaimed Yarghouz Barolass. "It is an honorable person in China, the grandson of an old man who babbled in his dotage, as old men often do, drooling secrets torture could not have wrung from him in his soundness of mind. The grandson, Yah Lai, has risen from a mean position to that of war-lord. He listened to the mumblings of his grandfather, a tooth-puller. He found a formula, written in code, and learned of symbols on the teeth of old men. He sent a request to me, with promise of much reward. I have one tooth, procured from the unfortunate person, Richard Lynch. Now if you will hand over the other--that of Job Hopkins--as you promised, perhaps we may reach a compromise by which Mr. Willoughby will be allowed to keep his life, in return for a tooth, as you hinted."

"As _I_ hinted?" exclaimed Rollins. "What are you driving at? I made no promise; and I certainly haven't Job Hopkins' tooth. You've got it, yourself."

"All this is unnecessary," objected Yarghouz, an edge to his tone. "You have a reputation for veracity, in spite of your violent nature. I was relying upon your reputation for honesty when I accepted this appointment. Of course, I already knew that you had Hopkins' tooth. When my blundering servants, having been frightened by you as they left the vaults, gathered at the appointed rendezvous, they discovered that he to whom was entrusted the jaw-bone containing the precious tooth, was not among them. They returned to the graveyard and found his body, but not the tooth. It was obvious that you had killed him and taken it from him."

Rollins was so thunderstruck by this new twist, that he remained speechless, his mind a tangled whirl of bewilderment.

Yarghouz Barolass continued tranquilly: "I was about to send my servants out in another attempt to secure you, when your agent phoned me--though how he located me on the telephone is still a mystery into which I must inquire-- and announced that you were ready to meet me at the House of Dreams, and give me Job Hopkins' tooth, in return for an opportunity to bargain personally for Mr. Willoughby's life. Knowing you to be a man of honor, I agreed, trusting you--"

"This is madness!" exclaimed Rollins "I didn't call you, or have anybody call you. _You,_ or rather, one of your men, called _me._"

"I did not!" Yarghouz was on his feet, his stocky body under the rippling black silk quivering with rage and suspicion. His eyes narrowed to slits, his wide mouth knotted viciously.

"You deny that you promised to give me Job Hopkins' tooth?"

"Sure I do!" snapped Rollins. "I haven't got it, and what's more, I'm not 'compromising' as you call it--"

"Liar!" Yarghouz spat the epithet like a snake hissing. "You have tricked--betrayed me--used my trust in your blackened honor to dupe me--"

"Keep cool," advised Rollins. "Remember, I've got a Colt .45 trained on you."

"Shoot and die!" retorted Yarghouz. "I do not know what your game is, but I know that if you shoot me, we will fall together. Fool, do you think I would keep my promise to a barbarian dog? Behind this hanging is the entrance to a tunnel through which I can escape before any of your stupid police, if you have brought any with you, can enter this room. You have been covered since you came through that door, by a man hiding behind the tapestry. Try to stop me, and you die!"

"I believe you're telling the truth about not calling me," said Rollins slowly. "I believe somebody tricked us both, for some reason. You were called, in my name, and I was called, in yours."

Yarghouz halted short in some hissing tirade. His eyes were like black evil jewels in the lamplight.

"More lies?" he demanded uncertainly.

"No; I think somebody in your gang is double-crossing you. Now easy, I'm not pulling a gun. I'm just going to show you the knife that I found sticking in the back of the fellow you seem to think I killed."

He drew it from his coat-pocket with his left hand--his right still gripped his gun beneath the garment--and tossed it on the divan.

Yarghouz pounced on it. His slit eyes flared wide with a terrible light; his yellow skin went ashen. He cried out something in his own tongue, which Rollins did not understand.

In a torrent of hissing sibilances, he lapsed briefly into English: "I see it all now! This was too subtle for a barbarian! Death to them all!" Wheeling toward the tapestry behind the divan he shrieked: "Gutchluk!"

There was no answer, but Rollins thought he saw the black velvety expanse billow slightly. With his skin the color of old ashes, Yarghouz Barolass ran at the hanging, ignoring Rollins' order to halt, seized the tapestries, tore them aside--something flashed between them like a beam of white hot light. Yarghouz's scream broke in a ghastly gurgle. His head pitched forward, then his whole body swayed backward, and he fell heavily among the cushions, clutching at the hilt of a skewer-like dagger that quivered upright in his breast. The Mongol's yellow claw-like hands fell away from the crimsoned hilt, spread wide, clutching at the thick carpet; a convulsive spasm ran through his frame, and those taloned yellow fingers went limp.

Gun in hand, Rollins took a single stride toward the tapestries--then halted short, staring at the figure which moved imperturbably through them: a tall yellow man in the robes of a mandarin, who smiled and bowed, his hands hidden in his wide sleeves.

"You killed Yarghous Barolass!" accused the detective.

"The evil one indeed has been dispatched to join his ancestors by my hand," agreed the mandarin. "Be not afraid. The Mongol who covered you through a peep-hole with an abbreviated shotgun has likewise departed this uncertain life, suddenly and silently. My own people hold supreme in the House of Dreams this night. All that we ask is that you make no attempt to stay our departure."

"Who are you?" demanded Rollins.

"But a humble servant of Fang Yin, lord of Peking. When it was learned that these unworthy ones sought a formula in America that might enable the upstart Yah Lai to overthrow the government of China, word was sent in haste to me. It was almost too late. Two men had already died. The third was menaced."

"I sent my servants instantly to intercept the evil Sons of Erlik at the vaults they desecrated. But for your appearance, frightening the Mongols to scattering in flight, before the trap could be sprang, my servants would have caught them all in ambush. As it was, they did manage to slay he who carried the relic Yarghouz sought, and this they brought to me."

"I took the liberty of impersonating a servant of the Mongol in my speech with you, and of pretending to be a Chinese agent of yours, while speaking with Yarghouz. All worked out as I wished. Lured by the thought of the tooth, at the loss of which he was maddened, Yarghouz came from his secret, well-guarded lair, and fell into my hands. I brought you here to witness his execution, so that you might realize that Mr. Willoughby is no longer in danger. Fang Yin has no ambitions for world empire; he wishes but to hold what is his. That he is well able to do, now that the threat of the devil-gas is lifted. And now I must be gone. Yarghouz had laid careful plans for his flight out of the country. I will take advantage of his preparations."

"Wait a minute!" exclaimed Rollins. "I've got to arrest you for the murder of this rat."

"I am sorry," murmured the mandarin. "I am in much haste. No need to lift your revolver. I swore that you would not be injured and I keep my word."

As he spoke, the light went suddenly out. Rollins sprang forward, cursing, fumbling at the tapestries which had swished in the darkness as if from the passing of a large body between them. His fingers met only solid walls, and when at last the light came on again, he was alone in the room, and behind the hangings a heavy door had been slid shut. On the divan lay something that glinted in the lamplight, and Rollins looked down on a curiously carven gold tooth.

THE END

www.ingramcontent.com/pod-product-compliance
Lightning Source LLC
Chambersburg PA
CBHW030241180626
46810CB00008B/3246